"Try these, Buddy," said Ziva Marie.

Ziva Marie ran straight to the shed and found
Momma's old wooden stilts.

"Momma and her sisters played on
these when they were little," she thought.
"I bet I can use them to make Charlie's legs longer
and his hands can be free."

"Charlie!" exclaimed Ziva Marie jumping up.
"You need legs like that!
And I know just what to do!"

"You can help me, Ziva Marie?"
Charlie asked hopefully.

Exasperated, they climbed
on the fence and wondered
what to do next.

"I need legs like that,"
mumbled Charlie.

The next morning Charlie attempted to feed the pigs on the tin can stilts.

Ziva Marie quickly realized that they did not solve the problem.
Charlie was once again showered in pig snorts and slobber.
The tin can stilts did make Charlie taller.
He could walk along the trough, and he could reach over the fence.
Just not at the same time.

"Ziva Marie," groaned Charlie. "The tin can stilts did not help me.
I need my hands to be free."

"Try these out, Charlie,"
said Ziva Marie.

"These are great." said Charlie.
"Thank you, Ziva Marie
for helping me!"

Ziva Marie worked and worked until
her project was complete.

"Charlie needs taller legs,"
Ziva Marie uttered to herself. "And I
think I know the perfect solution."

Ziva Marie got up and ran straight
to the barn. She found some rope
and scrounged through the
trash for empty cans.

"I…can't…keep…this…up,"
panted Ziva Marie.

"There must be a better way to
help you, Charlie!"

Ziva Marie could see that Charlie was not tall enough to hold the bucket over the fence and walk at the same time.

She picked him up and carried him along the trough while he dumped the feed.

Charlie tried and tried, but each time,
the feed dumped into one spot.

"My legs are too short," said Charlie.
"Ziva Marie, will you please help me?"

Ziva Marie beamed with pride watching Charlie lift the heavy bucket of feed and dump it into the feed trough.

"Remember to spread the feed out evenly so all the pigs can eat," said Ziva Marie.

The sun was rising over the farm when Ziva Marie and her little brother, Charlie, headed out.

"Now that I'm big, I can feed the piggies, right Ziva Marie?" asked Charlie.

"Yes! Today is your very first day!" answered Ziva Marie.

To our sweet, kindhearted, Ziva Marie.
Thank you for being the inspiration
for book number three!

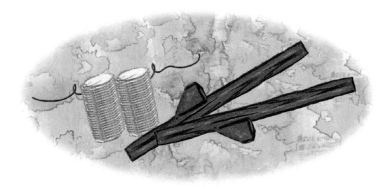

In Memory of our Grandma and Grandpa Alman.
Grandma inspired us to be who we are.
Grandpa created the wonderful stilts that we spent
hours playing on with our sisters.

PCS Engineers Publishing
1924 South Dan Jones Road
Avon, Indiana 46123
317-837-9900

Ordering information:
www.CreateSpace.com/6156681
www.amazon.com

Printed by CreateSpace, An Amazon.com Company

ISBN 978-0-9905344-2-6
Library of Congress Control Number: 2015949167

Book Layout and Design: Erin E. Norris-Güt
Fonts: Sassoon Primary, CurlzMT, Alegreya Sans Light,
PWSimpleHandwriting, Noteworthy, Impact

The illustrations in this book were made with watercolor. For
the "You Can Thanks to an Engineer," page, CAD was utilized
to create illustrations and graph paper was used for the
background.

First Edition, 2016

www.icanbeanengineer.com

You Can Count on Me!

I'm Ziva Marie!

written by: Cheryl A. Cunningham, PE and Judith E. Cunningham, MEd
illustrated by: Jill M. VanMatre, BSc

"They worked!" shouted Charlie.
"I'm taller, I can walk, and my
hands are free. Now I can
feed the pigs by myself!"

"Thank you, Ziva Marie,
for helping me!"

"Look at me!" laughed Charlie.
"I - have - robot - legs!"

"Let's go show everyone!"
exclaimed Ziva Marie.

"Look, Charlie! Here comes Dr. Chet, the vet. Hello, Dr. Chet!" greeted Ziva Marie.

"Hello, young lady and tall man," answered Dr. Chet. "I brought my son, Miles, today."

"Hello, Mr. Miles," welcomed
Ziva Marie and Charlie.
"Very nice to meet you!"

"Hey!" Charlie exclaimed.
"You look just like me!
You have robot legs too!"

"My legs are actually called prosthetics,"
explained Mr. Miles.
"But lots of people call them robot legs."

"Did your sister make them for you?"
Charlie asked.

"Yes she did," laughed Mr. Miles.
"She's an engineer."

"An engineer?" asked Ziva Marie.
"What is an engineer?"

"Engineers dream, imagine,
design and create," said Mr. Miles.
"That's what makes their job so great."

"I didn't have any legs before,
but now I can walk, run, dance, and so much more!
My artificial legs are like robots you see,
my sister, the engineer designed them for me."

"That sounds like something I can do.
I can make legs that help people too!"
exclaimed Ziva Marie.

She pranced and danced
and shouted with glee,
"When I grow up, I know what I'll be!"

Then climbing up high and grinning from ear to ear, Ziva Marie sang out her message in a voice loud and clear.

An Engineer, a Teacher, and an Artist

Sisters, Cheryl and Judy Cunningham, share a passion
for positively influencing children and youth.

As a professional engineer, Cheryl (the engineer) wanted
to introduce the fun and excitement of engineering by
demonstrating that problem solving in everyday activities is
what engineers do!

Cheryl is a licensed engineer in several states, including her
home state of Indiana. She received a Bachelor of Science
degree in Civil Engineering from Purdue University. She and
her husband own a civil engineering firm in Avon, Indiana.

As an educator, literacy advocate, and writer Judy (the
teacher) joined the team to create stories about
engineering for young children.

Judy received a Bachelor of Science degree in Early Childhood
Education from Georgia State University and a Master of
Science in Reading and Literacy from Walden University.
She currently resides in Arizona.

Judy's daughter, Jill VanMatre (the artist), captures
the essence of the stories with sketch, watercolor, and
technology.

Jill received her Bachelor of Science in Communications
with a minor in Drawing and Painting from Kennesaw
State University. She is a freelance photographer and
artist in Georgia.

You Can Count on Me! I'm Ziva Marie
is the third book in a collection of stories,
I Can Be An Engineer, written for young children.

The first two books in the series are available from Amazon.com.

You can

Ride your , walk your, watch,

play video games, your mom, to visit

grandma, take a to school, drink clean

water, take a, flush the, have clean

, play on the, go to the,

listen to, turn on a, eat an, work

on your, have lights in your, play

at night, with your friends,

and read this book...

...thanks to an Engineer!

Available on Amazon.com

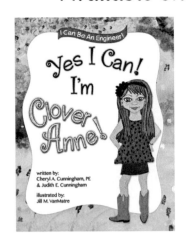 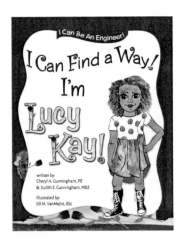

From the "I Can Be An Engineer" Series.

Coming soon to join the girls and their
engineering adventures!
Lydia Grace
The next character in the series,
"I Can Be An Engineer."

Made in the USA
San Bernardino, CA
09 April 2016